# GIRAFFE PROBLEMS

BY JORY JOHN ILLUSTRATED BY LANE SMITH

RANDOM HOUSE
NEW YORK

To Maria Modugno
—J.J. & L.S.

 Published in the United States by Random House
Children's Books, a division of Penguin Random House LLC, New York.
Random House and the colophon are registered trademarks of
Penguin Random House LLC.
Visit us on the Web! rhcbooks.com
Educators and librarians, for a variety of teaching tools, visit us at
RHTeachersLibrarians.com
Library of Congress Cataloging-in-Publication Data is available upon request.
ISBN 978-1-5247-7203-1 (trade) — ISBN 978-1-5247-7204-8 (lib. bdg.) —
ISBN 978-1-5247-7205-5 (ebook)
MANUFACTURED IN CHINA
10 9 8 7 6 5 4 3 2 1
First Edition
A tip of the hat to Nora Ephron
Random House Children's Books supports the First Amendment
and celebrates the right to read.

***Book design by Molly Leach***

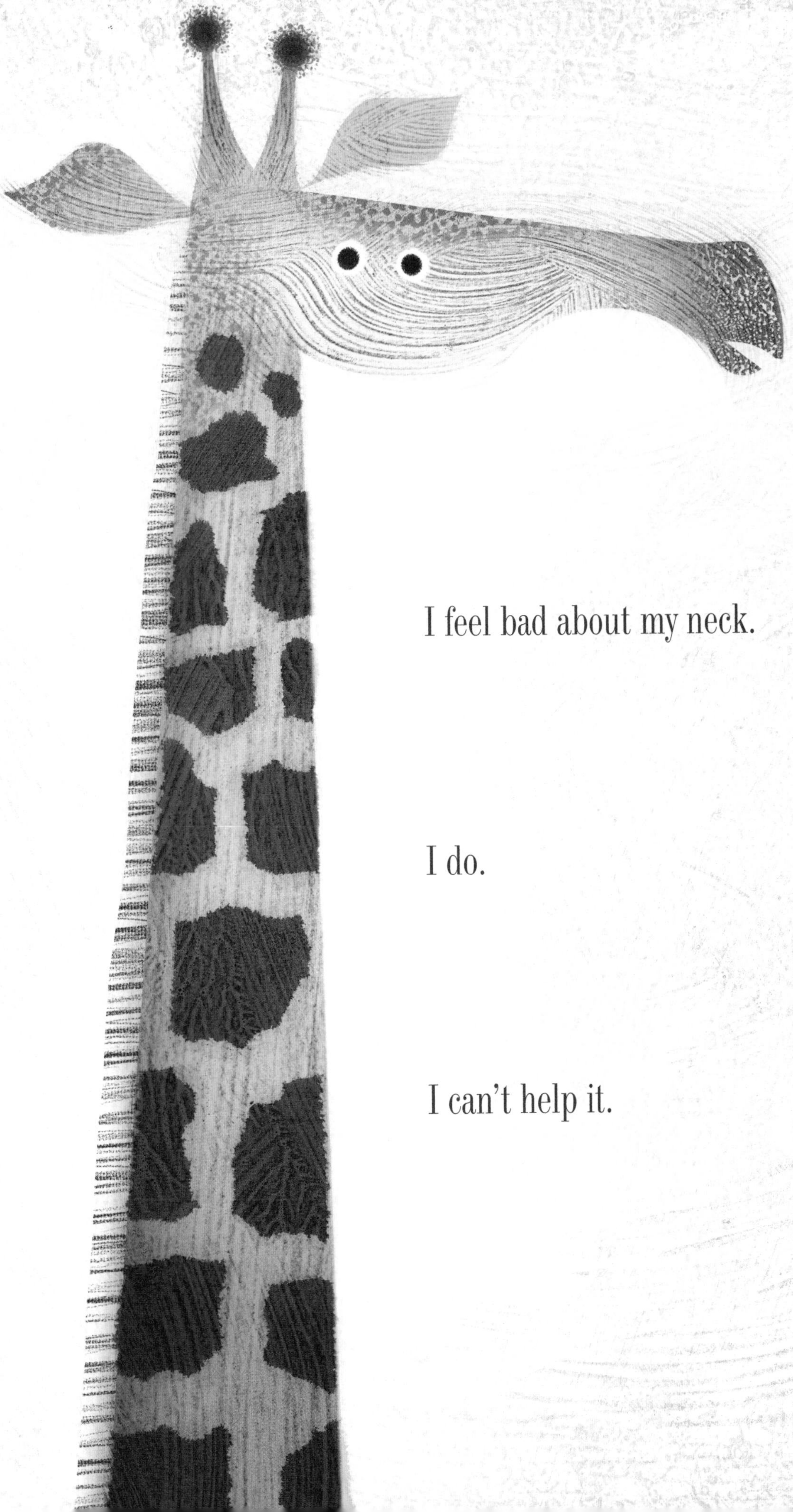

I feel bad about my neck.

I do.

I can't help it.

It's too long.

Too bendy.

Too narrow.

Too dopey.

Too patterned.

Too stretchy.

Too high.

Too lofty.

Too . . . *necky*.

Yes, my neck is too necky.

Everybody stares at it.

This guy.
Him.
That guy.

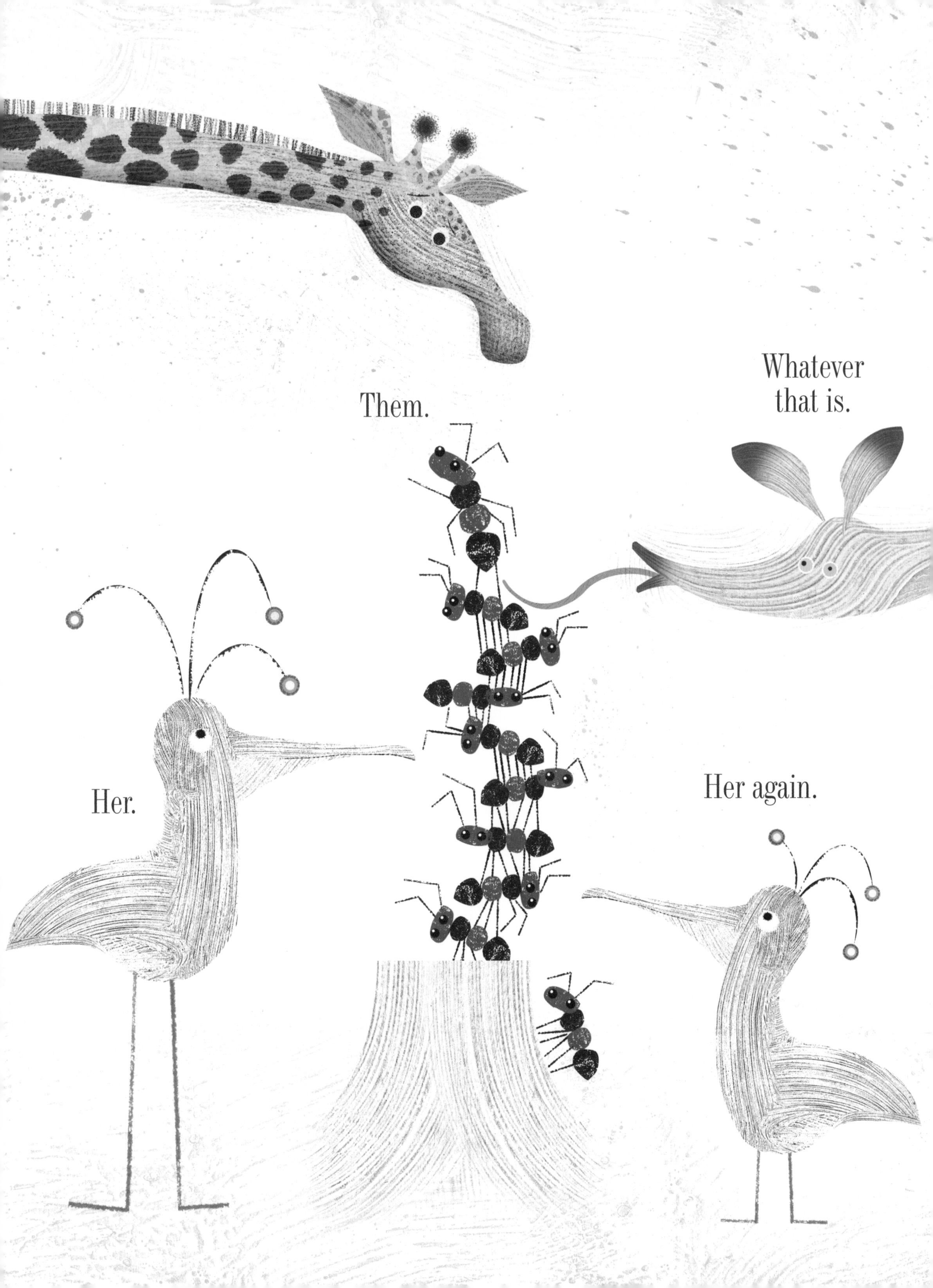
Her.
Them.
Whatever
that is.
Her again.

Yep, I feel bad about my neck.
I've tried dressing it up.

I've added a scarf.

Two scarves.

A bundle of scarves.

A *mountain* of scarves.

I’ve tried bow ties.

And regular ties.

And both.

I've tried hiding it away.
I've used shrubs.

I've hung out in ditches.

I’ve stood behind trees.

I’ve spent time in the river.

Other animals have necks that just . . . *work*.
Take a gander at this zebra's neck.
Stripes *always* look good.
So classic.

Quit staring at me.

Or gaze upon this elephant's neck.
Strong and powerful, yet graceful.

Stop talking about me.

Or glimpse this lion, whose neck is adorned
with a glorious mane of flowing locks.

What a sight!

How inspiring!

Why can't I have a neck like THAT?

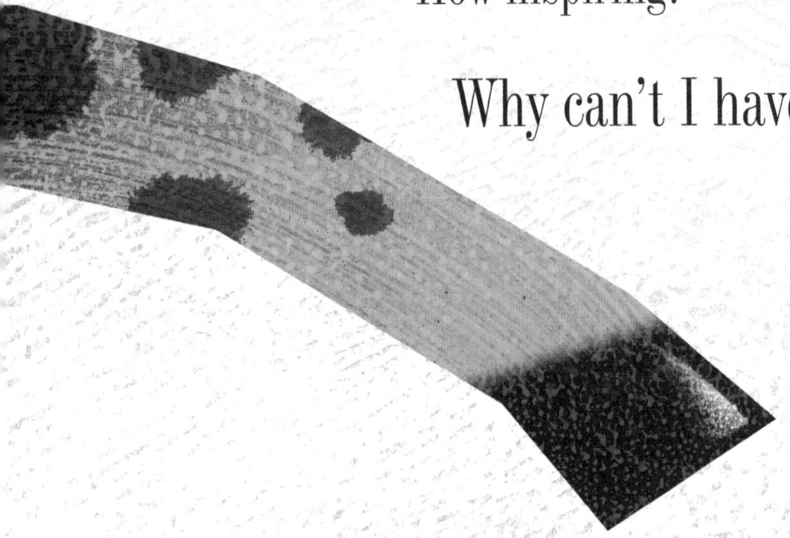

Are you *always* this loud?

My *mom* always said I should be *proud* of my neck.
She said other animals would *love* to have a neck like this.
Yeah, right.
No offense, Mom.
But *nobody* wants this neck.

It's a neck only a
mother could love.

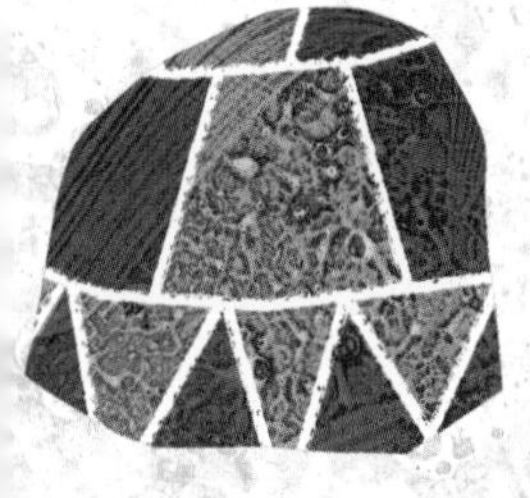

It all makes me want to hide until the sun sets.

Sheesh.

Good evening . . .

. . . I've been admiring your neck from afar.
Oh, how I wish *my* neck looked like yours!
I'd get so much done in a day.

Goodness, I can only *imagine* all the reaching
and grabbing and *looking around* I'd do.
I'd accomplish many of my goals, for sure.
Meanwhile, I'm saddled with *this* little
excuse for a neck.

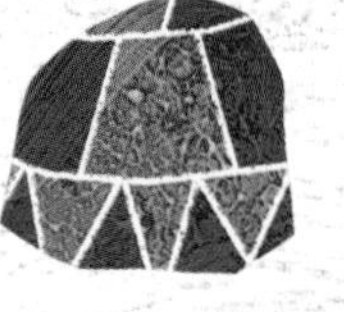

Here, watch me try to stretch it out.

See?
That’s about as far as it goes.
Pathetic, right? I’m basically neckless.

You feel bad about your neck, too?
Yep.
Huh.
I'm Cyrus, by the way.
I'm Edward.
It's lovely to
meet you, Cyrus.

Can I tell you something else, Edward?
Of course, Cyrus.

Ahem.

There is a hill in the distance, which you can

on that very hill for seven straight days now,

fruit—a lone banana!—slowly changed from

nights and unseasonably brisk mornings, with

hoping against hope that the fruit would drop

nourish myself in the process. Yet, day after

neck toward those greedy branches, only to

surely see from your great vantage. I've stood

staring skyward, watching as a single piece of

green to yellow, ripening. I've endured windy

very little sleep, as I waited . . . and *waited* . . .

before me so I could sample its sweetness and

day, I've felt like such a fool as I stretched my

be limited by my own physical shortcomings.

You want a banana from a tree?

That's what I said, yes.

PLUNK!

Here you go.

Oh! You did it! You made it look so easy!

*munch munch munch munch munch munch*

Delectable!
So that's what a banana tastes like, huh?
It was worth the wait!

Edward, face it—your neck is impressive.
It allows you to do amazing things.
For instance, you just solved my weeklong
banana dilemma in ten seconds.

Well . . . thank you, Cyrus.
I think you have a swell neck, too.
It's elegant and dignified,
and it works well with your shell.

That means a great deal to me, Edward.

I'm . . . I'm not *sure,* Edward.
I have very little experience with them.

You look wonderful, Cyrus!

As do you, Edward!

I feel good about our necks, Edward.

Thank you, Cyrus. For once, so do I. Yes, for once, so do I. . . .